THE GIRL ON THE HAT

Jane Jacobs

THE GIRL ON THE HAT

Illustrated by Karen Reczuch

Toronto
OXFORD UNIVERSITY PRESS
1989

For Caitlin and Larissa

Courtesy of Jimmy, Ned, and Burgin

Oxford University Press, 70 Wynford Drive, Don Mills, Ontario, M3C 1J9

Toronto Oxford New York Delhi Bombay Calcutta Madras Karachi
Petaling Jaya Singapore Hong Kong Tokyo Nairobi Dar es Salaam
Cape Town Melbourne Auckland

and associated companies in
Berlin Ibadan

CANADIAN CATALOGUING IN PUBLICATION DATA

Jacobs, Jane, 1916–
The girl on the hat

ISBN 0-19-540708-3

I. Reczuch, Karen. II. Title.

PS8569.A26G57 1989   jC813'.54   C89-093470-3
PZ7.J326Gi 1989

OXFORD is a trademark of Oxford University Press
1234-2109

CONTENTS

1

The Boat Ride

Tina was a little little girl. If she curled up and scrunched her toes she could fit in a peanut shell. Her real name was Ernestina but when her parents and her brother Ernest saw how small she was they began calling her Peanutina. But then that took too long to say, so mostly they called her Tina.

Next to peanut shells, Tina's best things were hats. Her mother would say, "Let's go out," and Tina would race across the floor, take a big jump and grab the hem of her mother's coat. She would scramble up the cloth, resting a moment at the belt. Then up again, another jump from her mother's shoulder, and there she was on the hat.

It was a pretty sight in a snowstorm to see Tina snuggled in the warm brown fuzzy hat behind the hatband, sticking out her tongue to catch snow flakes. She could scrape up snow from the hat and make snowballs to throw at other people's hats. When one of her little snowballs hit somebody Tina would giggle so hard her mother would say, "Tina, calm down. You are giving me a headache with all that giggling up there on my head."

Next to hats, Tina's best things were strings and cords. She swung on the cord that came out of the telephone. She swung on the vacuum cleaner cord in the midst of all the delicious rumble when her mother cleaned up the crumbs on the carpet.

Ernest hung ribbons and strings from the coat hooks by the front door so she could climb them and jump off into pillows.

One summer day when Tina was in the park with her father and Ernest, she looked up and saw a red kite with a long white string. She studied the kite thoughtfully, and then the boy who was holding the string. Maybe he would let her climb up it until she reached the kite. She could fly with it. It would be her airplane.

But Tina's father looked up at the kite too and he knew just what Tina was thinking. "No, no," he said. "We don't want you to fall from high up. You must promise me, no kites."

Tina tried to argue with him. "I wouldn't let go," she said. "I would be safe."

"I know you could hang on," said her father. "But the wind plays too many tricks."

"All right, I promise," said Tina sadly.

"Let's go for a boat ride," said her father. "I will row and you can ride on Ernest's cap. Hang tight to the button on top."

Tina had never been on a boat ride and neither had Ernest. Tina drummed her feet in excitement on Ernest's cap while her father bought the ticket. The ticket woman saw her and said, "Here, here, give back that ticket. No babies allowed in the boats."

Ernest said, "This is no baby! My sister is seven years old and she can read and write."

"I want to be big like other people," Tina said as they waited at the boat dock.

"We like you fine the way you are," said Ernest.

"You are just right for you," said her father. "Don't

2

worry about your size." Tina still wished she were bigger but she felt happy anyway, thinking about the boat ride.

When they got in the boat, Ernest and Tina begged to sit in the prow because it was pointy and in front. "Very well, said their father, "But you must behave because my back will be turned while I'm rowing. You must watch and tell me if we're going to bump into anything. Sit quietly and don't jiggle the boat."

It was exciting leaving the dock. "To the right!" Ernest called and they just missed bumping another rowboat. "Left!" screeched Tina and they slipped safely past a canoe. "Good navigators," said their father.

A hat is a good place for seeing most things but Tina wanted to look more closely at the water. When Ernest leaned over to snatch a stick floating by, Tina slid down his back to the seat and perched on the edge of the boat. Ernest did not notice.

Now everybody's back was turned to Tina. She leaned way over the side to watch the water going slap, slap against the boat. An old paper cup floated by. It bumped the boat and began to sink. Tina leaned over even farther to watch it go under the water. She leaned too far and tried to wiggle back but it was too late. Over the side of the boat she went.

Splash! She hit the water and sank. The boat moved on and when Tina came to the top of the water and lifted her head it was far away.

"I must find a boat of my own," she thought, "or this will be the end of me." A wave swept over her and she squeezed her eyes shut and thrashed her arms. Her hand hit something and she grabbed it. When she opened her eyes, she found it was a peanut shell.

Over the side of the peanut shell scrambled Tina. It was a perfect little boat. It even had a seat in the middle and a deep place for her feet. She remembered how Ernest had grabbed a stick from the water so she watched in the hope she would find oars. A toothpick drifted near, and then a little twig. She bit two nicks in the peanut shell for oarlocks.

She aimed her boat toward the nearest land—a tiny island made of one rock, one clump of moss, three green reeds and somebody's old sandwich. Her voyage was hard and dangerous. A canoe almost ran over her and she heard a little girl shout, "Stop! Stop! A little tiny girl in a little tiny boat!" But they thought she was making it up and did not stop.

Only a few minutes after Tina fell into the water, Ernest pointed down and said, "See, Tina, a little fish." When she didn't answer he reached up to his cap and couldn't find her. Then he carefully took off the cap. No, she wasn't there. "Tina is gone!" he cried.

His father let go of the oars. He and Ernest searched the boat. Then in great fright they looked at the pond, but they hardly knew where to look first. They felt desperate.

They heard a girl shout, "Stop! Stop! A little tiny girl in a little tiny boat!" So they looked and looked over the water for a little boat of some sort but they could not see one.

Tina's arms ached from rowing. Her hands were sore. But she did not dare stop and drift.

At last she came to shore upon the sandwich and rested. Then she dragged the boat onto the moss beside the reeds. She managed to bend down one of the reeds and hang her sweater on it. When she let go, the

4

reed sprang back up and the sweater fluttered in the breeze.

Her shipwreck flag caught her father's eye. Then he saw Tina standing under it. She was waving wildly to them.

Her father and Ernest hugged her and kissed her. "Show us your boat," said her father. Tina got into the peanut shell again and rowed once around the little island, so proud that she forgot her hands were sore.

"You are brave Peanutina in your peanut shell," said Ernest. "Brave tiny Tina," said her father. But Tina did not feel so brave any longer. She wanted to feel safe now.

"Let Ernest row," she said to her father. "I want to ride in your shirt pocket."

Ernest got a rowing lesson from both of them all the way back. When they walked past the ticket booth the ticket woman called out angrily, "She is even smaller than a baby!"

Tina giggled and Ernest said, "My sister can row a boat better than anybody!"

Their father said, "Don't stop and talk, Ernest. We have to hurry home now and pack for our big bus trip tomorrow."

2

The Cave

Tina's uncle and aunt and her American cousin Jerry lived far away on a peanut farm in Kentucky. That was where Tina and her family were going, to give Ernest and Tina a taste of farm life.

The trip in the bus was wonderful. All the passengers wanted to let Tina ride on their hats. At the end of their trip the driver said she could ride on his hat. She was the first person her uncle and aunt and Jerry saw when the bus drove into the station.

It was peanut harvesting time. Tina's father and Ernest said they would help. The way it was done, they pulled at the peanut vines with rakes. The vines grew along the ground but the peanuts grew under the ground. When the rakes pulled at the vines, up came the peanuts too, looking like little clumps of hairy dirt. Later the peanuts would be cut off and cleaned and roasted and maybe some of the shells would finally drop into the boat pond in the city.

Tina wanted to help too but her parents thought it was too dangerous because of the sharp rakes and the truck her uncle drove back and forth in the fields, picking up loads of vines.

"I'm going to unpack our bags," her mother said. "Later I will take you for a nice walk, Tina. You play on the porch for now. Don't wander away."

For a while Tina made little houses out of peanut shells and crawled under them. Then she sat quietly in

7

one of her little houses, peering out and thinking. She was thinking of a cave Jerry had talked about on the ride from the bus station. It was just over the hill from their house, he said. It wandered so far under the ground nobody had been to the end of it. People could get lost there.

"I will not get lost," thought Tina. "I will take a string and find my way back by following the string." She knew this would work. She had read about it in a book.

Softly she crept into the house and climbed over the side of her aunt's sewing basket. She wound red thread around and around her waist until she looked like a spool of thread herself, with a head and arms and legs sticking out. Then she slipped out the door, through the fence and up the hill.

A hawk saw her and thought she was a mouse, good to eat. Tina drew the sword with which she had armed herself for her adventure. It was only a pin but she waved it and shouted war cries. The hawk changed its mind because it had never seen a mouse flashing a silver sword and making a racket like that.

Without further trouble Tina reached the cave. She tied the end of the thread to the pin and pushed it securely into the ground. Then she entered the cave, unwinding as she went.

The cave looked like a fairyland castle. She drank from a little pool where water dripped from a spike of rock overhead. The pool shone with purple, gleamed with red and glittered with white. "Wow!" said Tina.

Dancing and unwinding, she came to another pool and was surprised that it looked dark and gloomy instead of bright and beautiful. Then she noticed the whole cave was getting dark. Far behind her was its

sunny opening. Ahead it was so dark she could not see.

Tina knew she should go back now. But she still had quite a bit of thread. "I will go to the end of the string," she said out loud. Her words echoed back from the sides of the cave as if many people had spoken.

That was fun, so as she moved along in the dark taking careful little steps and keeping her hand on the side of the cave, she barked like a dog and meowed like a cat and mooed like a cow. The barking echoes mixed with the meowing and mooing echoes and sometimes she shouted "Woweeeee!"

Then suddenly, louder than the echoes, came a great roar behind her. The whole cave rumbled and shook. In the noise was the smell of dust. Tina crouched down in fear for a long time. She kept very quiet, in case there was a giant in the cave, or a troll, or a lion.

At last, when everything was still, she began to feel her way back along the thread. But soon she felt something lying on the thread. It was a small stone. How did that get there, she wondered.

Only a few steps farther a huge rock was on the string. Feeling her way around it, Tina could not find the thread again. She tugged the piece of thread in her hand and it came loose. It was broken off.

Now Tina understood what had made the great noise. It wasn't a monster. Part of the cave had fallen in. It blocked her way. Try as she might, she could not get through the big piles of rocks or see any crack of light ahead. In the dark, now and again a stone rolled from the pile.

Tina was very frightened. Suppose a rolling stone

should crush her. Suppose more of the cave fell down. She knew she would have to find some other way out.

With her thread no use to her, Tina just kept moving deeper into the cave, feeling her way along the wall. Whenever she felt an opening and wondered whether she should go in it or go past it, she said "Eeny, meeny, miney, mo."

But then she stopped and thought, this will not do. "I am under the ground," she said to herself. "I want to get up on the ground. I should feel if a place is going uphill. If it is, that is where I should go."

That is what she did. In this way, always trying to go uphill, finally she found herself in a tunnel that was getting smaller and smaller. It got so small that even Tina could not stand up in it and she began to crawl.

Little roots stuck out from the sides. In the darkness she felt them and used them to pull herself up the steep places. This little tunnel was dirt, not rock, and Tina dug away the narrow sides with her hands as she moved along.

Then she came to something blocking her way. Maybe this was as far as she could go. But before she gave up and tried to crawl back, she decided to try digging her way around the thing. It felt like a hard hairy lump. It reminded her of something. "Why, it's a peanut! I won't starve!" She grabbed hold of the peanut.

Suddenly, in a shatter of dirt and light, Tina felt herself and the peanut being lifted high in the air. She held on with all her might and closed her eyes. Then she felt herself and her peanut dropping and she landed in a springy, scratchy bunch of something.

Tina opened her eyes and found herself looking

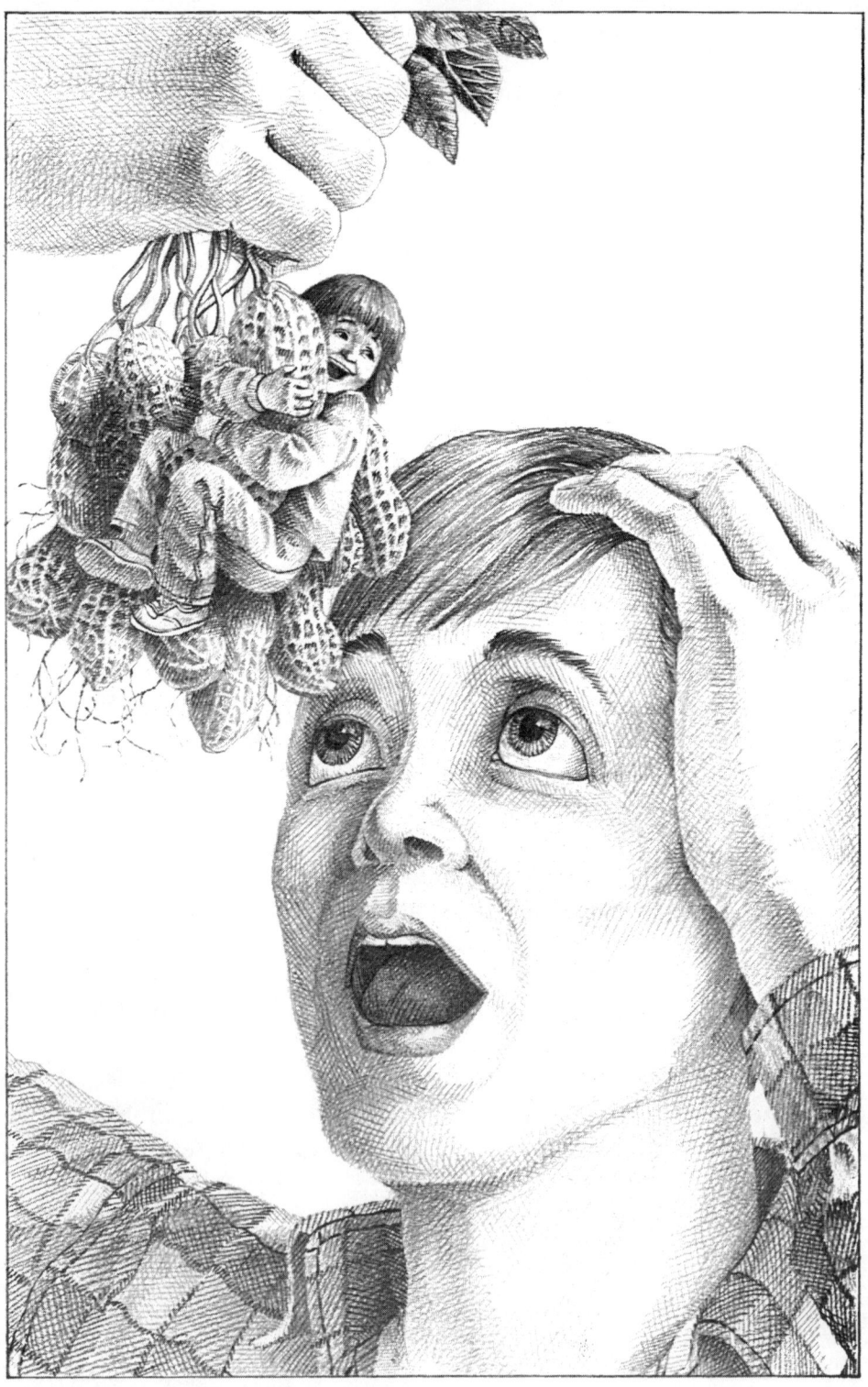

straight into her father's eyes. He dropped his rake and said, "Tina! How in the world did you come up with these peanuts?"

The next morning Tina and all the others went off to the cave. At the opening Tina showed them the pin in the ground with her red thread still tied to it. She showed them the bright pool of water. Then they followed the thread to the cave-in. No one could go farther.

"You are an explorer," said Ernest. "You are the last explorer of the rest of this cave."

3

Kidnapped

On the way home from Kentucky a dreadful thing happened. Tina's mother put her hat upside down on the seat beside her so Tina could nap comfortably inside it. While Tina was asleep and her mother was looking out the window a sly woman walked up the aisle, scooped Tina from the hat, tucked her quickly in her purse, got off the bus and hurried away.

The woman, whose name was Eggy Wimpoodle, worked in a carnival show that was run by her partner, Slap the Fleaman.

Slap's show was a box with seven little dead fleas in it. Eggy had dressed up the fleas to look like a bride and groom and five bridesmaids. People paid Slap fifty cents to look through a magnifying glass at the fleas in their tiny perfect clothes. They said, "For goodness sake. Imagine that. Look at their clothes."

When Eggy opened her purse and showed Slap what she had, he was delighted. "We'll make our fortune with this little freak."

"I am not a freak," said Tina. "I'm seven years old and I can read and write and row a boat and explore a—"

"Shut up!" said Slap and he dumped her back in Eggy's purse and snapped it shut.

Tina did not get out of that purse all day. They dropped her a piece of popcorn now and then, and dribbled into her mouth a few drops from the bottoms of their orange pop bottles, and Eggy said, "I'm busy." That was all.

As soon as Tina's mother realized Tina was not in the hat she called her name. No answer. Everyone in the bus began to call her and they searched everywhere. Nobody knew how she could have left the bus but she wasn't there. So the driver stopped again and Tina's mother and father and Ernest got off. The bus went on without them.

Tina's father called the Bureau of Missing Persons from a phone booth outside a lunch counter. "My seven-year-old daughter is missing," he told the man who answered the phone. "She is two inches tall and—"

"You mean four feet and two inches tall," the man said.

"No, she is unusually small," said Tina's father. "Two inches, and I am afraid—"

"Listen, wise guy," said the man, "We're busy people here with no time for jokes. If you lost a doll call Lost and Found," and he hung up. A tear rolled down Tina's father's cheek.

"Let me handle this, dear," said Tina's mother. "You and Ernest wait at the lunch counter and I will go to the Bureau of Missing Persons."

Tina's mother told the man who sat at the desk, "I wish to report a lost child. Age, seven years. Wearing blue jeans, a yellow T-shirt, yellow socks and little red sandals."

The man wrote all that down. Then he asked, "Color of hair? Color of eyes? Height? Weight?"

"Brown hair," said Tina's mother and the man wrote that down. "Hazel eyes," and the man wrote that

down. "Two inches tall." The man stopped writing.

"You're the second nut we've heard from today," he said. "Is this some kind of a joke? Look lady, stop bothering us, give your imagination a rest." While he was saying this he led Tina's mother out the door and slammed the door shut.

Back at the lunch counter Tina's parents and Ernest had a conference. Tina's mother thought they should find a room in a hotel or motel near by and keep searching from there. "But we don't know where to search," said Tina's father. "This is terrible."

Ernest tried to keep their spirits up. "Remember the boat ride?" he said. "Remember the cave?" Tina has been in trouble before and gotten out of it. I think she'll find her way home this time."

"If we're in a strange hotel here, she won't know how to find us," said Tina's father. "She will think we're lost too."

They decided the best thing they could do was go home where Tina would expect them to be. But of course they were sad and worried and wondered if they would ever find her again.

Tina, huddled up in Eggy's purse, was sad and worried too.

4

The Carnival

Tina could hardly move in Eggy's purse. It was stuffed with Kleenex and old shopping lists along with pencils, cloth samples, a lipstick, keys, sticks of chewing gum and lots of slippery dimes and quarters. Most of the time the whole mess was bouncing and jouncing and so was Tina. Whenever Eggy set the purse down, Tina just kept still.

But finally the purse stayed still a long time and Tina began to rummage through it. She felt each object in the dark. Near the bottom she came to Eggy's eyebrow tweezers.

Tina went right to work with the tweezers. She pried a little hole through the side of the purse. Then she ripped the hole bigger. After peeping out and seeing nothing, she wiggled out.

She found she was on a dirty wooden floor inside a tent. It was not very light so Tina realized it must be night now. She peeped around the purse and saw a chair leg. Eggy was sitting in the chair, underneath a hanging light bulb. She had a heap of green wool in her lap and she was knitting so fast her fingers danced.

"There," Eggy was saying. "The sweater's almost done. Now all that's left is the pillow."

"Hurry up," Slap grumbled. He was sitting on a wooden platform, tapping his fingers on a big doll house beside him. "You're so slow, Eggy. Hurry up, hurry up, hurry up."

Tina waited until Slap was busy putting the little

green sweater in the doll house and Eggy was busy threading a needle. Then she crawled behind Eggy's chair to the edge of the floor. She pushed up the bottom of the tent a tiny bit and wiggled under.

At last she was outside. But where was she?

Tina had never been to a carnival. She had never even heard of a carnival. There were tents and stands stretching as far as she could see. Crowds of people roved everywhere. They clutched huge stuffed animals. They pushed and pulled each other this way and that. They shrieked and squealed.

Tina heard bangs and bells and shouts from the tents and stands. She heard thumps and whacks, harsh music, and machines clanking and grinding. She smelled hot dogs and hamburgers. She smelled popcorn and horses. Everywhere lights dazzled and glittered, all colors and sizes of lights, swaying and flashing. They made people's faces look green sometimes, or violet. The ground around Tina was a jumble of half-eaten candy apples, broken drippy ice cream cones and stepped-on boxes.

Tina shrank back against the tent canvas. She thought all these people were crazy. She thought they lived in the tents like Eggy and Slap.

Near her a little boy let go of his balloon by mistake. He began to cry. His mother scolded him for losing his balloon and he cried harder. Tina wished she were clinging to the balloon string, making her getaway.

As she watched the lost balloon rising, she noticed that in the sky people were traveling back and forth. They were sitting in moving sky-seats. She squinted and saw the moving seats were hanging from high cables. She did not know where the people were going. She thought they were leaving this crazy tent city. She saw that the sky cables began at a high bright tower near by.

So Tina took a big breath to make herself feel brave and headed toward the tower, keeping to the sides of tents where she could and dashing across the walks when she saw her chance.

Now that she knew where she was going she began to like the carnival. She saw that most children held onto their balloons and were laughing. That made her laugh too.

At the tower she sneaked into an elevator and huddled in a corner behind the other passengers. Everybody got off at the sky-ride platform and so did Tina.

Nobody noticed Tina sneaking up to a waiting seat. Nobody noticed she was hitching a free ride on the pipe framework behind the seat. A moment later three people got into that seat, the door slammed, and the seat started moving.

This was fun. On her perch high over the carnival Tina felt she was truly free. She sang out loud,

> Slap and Eggy can't catch me
> Yah, yah
> They can't catch me.

Down below her the carnival lights looked beautiful. The distant noise was exciting. The music and shouts sounded jolly. A balloon drifted so close that Tina leaned out and reached with one hand to catch the string.

Just then all the sky seats jolted to a stop because more people were getting on at the tower. Tina did not expect the jolt. It made her let go and fall.

Down she went, but she didn't hit the ground. She landed PLOP in a big, foamy, squashy, soft pink blob of cotton candy that somebody was eating. When Tina opened her eyes the first thing she saw was a tongue. It had licked the cotton candy off her face.

The tongue belonged to Eggy. Eggy screamed and dropped her cotton candy. Then she grabbed at it and fell down. Tina landed in her lap, and so did the cotton candy all down the front of Eggy's dress. Eggy yelled, "Slap! Quick! Look! I found her!"

Slap was stuffing his mouth with maplenut fudge. With his sticky hand he grabbed sticky Tina from Eggy's sticky lap and ran to the tent. It was just around the corner from the candy stand.

Tina licked the candy off her hands. Eggy washed off the rest at a drinking fountain and after the bath put a little nightgown on Tina.

"You won't get away again, you little freak," said Slap. He popped Tina into the doll house. All Tina noticed in there was a little brass bed with a patchwork quilt and a pillow. But before she fell asleep she began thinking of ways to fool Slap and Eggy.

5

The Escape

The big doll house was really a cage. When Tina woke in the morning she saw the house had windows all along the front and two sides, but no door. Her bed was in one corner. In another corner was a little wooden table and a chair. Between them, across the back of the house was a long built-in closet. In the closet Tina found an old-fashioned dress with pink ruffles, a pair of brown slacks and the sweater she had seen Eggy knitting. There was also a yellow raincoat and a brown umbrella painted with tiny yellow daffodils. Everything was just her size.

While Tina was fooling with the umbrella to see if it worked, Eggy opened the roof of the house. The roof was really a lid, with a hinge like the lid of a box. Eggy put some popcorn and a thimble of orange pop on the table. She told Tina that people were going to pay to watch her through the windows.

"Your job," Eggy said, "Is a fashion show. You have to change clothes very fast in that closet and then show off your outfits. The last thing, you put on the raincoat and open up that little umbrella and twirl it and strut around."

Eggy made Tina practice the fashion show all morning. Slap told her she wouldn't get anything to eat unless she smiled and did it right.

As soon as people are watching me, thought Tina, I will bang on a window and yell, "Help! Save me! I have been kidnapped! Inform my parents!"

But this was not to be. The instant Tina ran to a window all the lights went out. Nobody could see her. Slap had pushed the light switch. She could hear him saying, "Sorry, folks, we have a little problem. Step outside please and wait while repairs are made."

Then the top of the cage swung open and Slap said, "No more food today. Don't try any more monkey business or you won't get food from now on. Understand?"

"But I'll starve," said Tina.

"Shut up!" said Slap.

So Tina did the fashion show over and over. That night, hungry and angry, she cried herself to sleep.

In the morning she had another plan. She would write KIDNAPPED and stick the sign inside the umbrella where people could read it when she twirled and strutted.

"Please, may I have a paper and pencil?" asked Tina when Slap opened the cage to see that she was up.

"No!" said Slap, "Shut up!" and he slammed down the roof.

When it opened again for Eggy to put Tina's breakfast of popcorn and pop on the table, Tina said, "Well, can I just have a peanut? Please, I need it for exercise. I can jump on and off and roll it around."

"Oh, let her have the peanut," said Eggy. "I'll make her a little jogging outfit and it can be part of the show."

That night when everything was dark and quiet and they thought she was asleep, Tina slipped out of bed and put the peanut into bed instead. She tucked the quilt around it and left just a little bit of peanut shell showing so it would look like her cheek against the pillow.

Then she put on the slacks and sweater and laid the umbrella on the table. Making not a sound, she climbed on the table herself. Next she lifted the chair up on the table and climbed on the chair, taking the umbrella with her. Standing on the chair, she was up near the ceiling of the little room. If she gave herself a push she could reach the top of the wall when the roof was opened.

Then she sat down on the chair and dozed a little and waited till morning.

Finally morning came and Slap opened the roof. Quick as a flash, Tina threw the umbrella over the wall. It fell on the platform below her cage. She pulled herself to the top of the wall and like lightning she slid down outside to the platform right beside the umbrella. She opened it up and used it for a parachute to jump to the ground. Then she ran toward the door of the tent, right past Slap's feet.

The reason Slap did not see all this was that he was talking to the peanut in the bed. "Get up!" he growled. "Get up, you lazy thing!"

Of course the peanut did not move. "Answer me!" he yelled. "Say something!" Of course the peanut did not answer.

Slap was furious. He reached in to push Tina out of bed and of course only a peanut rolled out.

Then Slap turned around and saw Tina racing out of the tent. He started to run after her. But Eggy had heard Slap growling and yelling and she came running to see what was the matter. She ran bang into Slap. They both fell down, both screaming at each other, "Why don't you look where you're going?"

While this disgraceful hullabaloo was going on, Tina kept running and found herself in a crowd of people waiting for tents to open. Afraid she would be

trampled, Tina jumped onto a brown loafer and began pulling at the white sock above it.

The loafer and sock belonged to a girl named Lucy Dansy who was eight years old and had come to the carnival with her mother. When Lucy leaned down to see what was bothering her sock her long hair fell all around Tina like a curtain. That was lucky because now Slap was searching outside for Tina and coming close. But when he looked in her direction all he saw was Lucy Dansy's long hair.

Softly Tina whispered in Lucy's ear. "Don't say anything. Just put me in your pocket and take me away. I have been kidnapped."

Lucy was a sensible girl, and a giggler, like Tina. Giggling, she gently scooped Tina into her pocket. With her other hand she tugged at her mother's slacks and said, "Let's go home. Don't ask why, I'll show you later."

At Lucy's house, Lucy and her mother gave Tina a good meal of chicken soup with rice. While she was eating they telephoned Tina's parents long distance. Her parents immediately went to the airport to reach Tina as fast as possible.

Then Lucy's mother called the police and told them about the kidnapping. They arrested Slap at the carnival where he was packing away the doll house, and then they asked Tina if she had anything special to say about him.

"Yes, I do," said Tina. "If he asks for a pencil and paper don't give it to him."

Eggy tried to run away to the woods but the police soon found her. They asked Tina if she had anything to say about Eggy.

"Yes, I do," said Tina. "If you get her a job making jackets for teddy bears she might live a useful life. But she is sly. Keep an eye on her."

The man from the Bureau of Missing Persons came to Lucy's house too. He apologized to Tina and her parents.

On the way home in the airplane, Tina's father said, "Tina, you have been in a lot of trouble lately. It is time to think how to stay out of trouble and how you can lead a useful life too. What would you like to do at home for the rest of this summer?"

6

Finding Work

Thinking about a useful life for herself, Tina's first idea was to make little Easter baskets, starting a long time ahead to have plenty to sell by next Easter. She put ten empty peanut shells out in a row. She lined them with sweet-smelling dried basil and filled them with red cranberries, blueberries and green peas. They looked like darling little nests of tiny colored eggs. But in a few days the berries spoiled and the peas began to shrivel.

"Why don't you use beads?" asked Tina's mother. "In my top drawer is a box of loose beads. Pick out what you want."

As Tina rummaged around in the box she thought how pretty it was in the drawer. The light shone down through colored scarves that Tina's mother dropped in the drawer without folding, and it glittered on necklaces that lay at the bottom. It was almost as beautiful as the cave. It was prettier than the carnival lights. But then Tina picked out her beads and got back to work on the baskets.

After she filled ten baskets, she started on ten more. But by that time she was sick and tired of making Easter baskets. "This is boring," she said. "I am through with it."

"Why don't you make peanut-shell boats with sails?" asked Ernest. Tina thought about making twenty peanut-shell boats and sails. She said, "Yuk!"

"Why don't you make painted peanut-shell neck-laces?" asked her mother. "You could paint each one differently."

"Why don't you make little peanut-shell teddy bears?" asked her father.

But Tina had been thinking about the bureau drawer. She said, "I wish I had a little camera so I could take pictures inside of bureau drawers. Nobody but me knows how it looks there, down underneath the things on top. If I could take pictures everybody could see what I see."

The next Saturday they all went off to the biggest camera store and bought the tiniest camera. It was almost as big as Tina but she could handle it because she was so strong from climbing and running and jumping. It even had a tiny automatic flash bulb.

Tina practiced with it by taking pictures of peanuts on the dining room table while everybody gave her advice.

Then she was ready to take it into her mother's top bureau drawer. She could hardly wait for those pictures to be developed. Some were blurry and some didn't show much except the wooden sides of the drawer, but three were wonderful. Everyone said, "Take more!"

So next Tina took pictures in a drawer that looked as if it were only full of tangles of string. But underneath was a jumble of old keys, a screwdriver, three ping-pong balls and a bunch of paper roses. These things looked interesting under the string tangles. Then she poked around in the kitchen cupboards. She photographed the flour sifter under a muffin tin.

The next cupboard had boxes. To Tina they looked

something like buildings along narrow streets and alleys.

Tina turned a corner around a cornstarch box and came face-to-face with a mouse. It had gnawed a hole right through the cardboard. Its teeth looked dangerous to Tina as they glittered behind the white cornstarch on its whiskers and nose. The mouse was just about as big as Tina and so close. She was afraid, but she also thought what a wonderful picture and she snapped the camera.

The bright automatic flash on the camera went off. The startled mouse jumped out of the cupboard and ran behind the refrigerator.

Ernest sent the picture of the mouse with cornstarch on its face to the natural history magazine and they said they would print it. Now Tina knew just what kind of work she wanted to do while leading a useful life. She wanted to go down into animal holes, the way she had gone into small passages in the cave. "I will take pictures of animals in their own homes," she said. "While they are startled by the flash, I will turn around and run. I will be Peanutina, The Animal Photographer. No, I will be Ernestina, The Animal Photographer."

7

The Weasels

Tina's mother thought hard about how to protect Tina in animal holes. She was worried about stings from yellow jackets and hornets. After much searching and shopping she found some special cloth that was thin but so strong and tough a stinger would not go through. She sent the cloth by mail to Eggy and asked her to make Tina a coverall with a hood.

By this time Eggy was as sick and tired of making teddy bear jackets as Tina had been of making Easter baskets. She was glad to make the coverall with a hood, and then she made little gloves and strong little hiking boots and even goggles.

Well equipped, Tina took her camera down into the hole of a field mouse in the small park near her house. She photographed its nest of babies. On Saturdays she traveled out to fields and woods with Ernest and crawled into burrows of rabbits, moles and ground-hogs. She climbed down into hollow trees where squirrels made their nests. She wiggled into damp hollows of fallen logs and took pictures of slugs and snails.

One Saturday afternoon Tina saw a hole near the bank of a stream. It looked as if it belonged to a rabbit family. Down the hole she went, expecting a long-eared rabbit who would be frightened when the camera flashed.

This time it was Tina who had a bad fright. When

the flash went off she saw a strange dark brown animal with flat little ears and a huge mouth filled with sharp, sharp teeth. It lunged at Tina. Its teeth tore her gloves and scraped the ends of her fingers before she could pull them away. Tina dropped her camera in front of the fierce mouth and ran. All she cared about was getting out of the hole alive.

When Ernest saw Tina rushing from the hole sobbing and with her fingers bleeding, he sat down and put her on his knee. First he cut tiny band-aids from a regular band-aid he kept in his pocket first-aid kit, and gently put them on her fingers. He was frightened too by her narrow escape and said they should go home.

But Tina did not want to go without her camera. So they decided to wait until they saw the animal come out of the hole. "Then you can keep watch for me," said Tina, "while I go back down for the camera."

Hiding behind a fallen log and keeping very still, both Ernest and Tina watched the hole until their eyes were so tired they could hardly look any longer. Then they took turns watching. The log and the forest around them smelled sweet and damp, but they felt dry and stiff and itchy. At last, when the sun was going down, Ernest was about to say they would have to go without the camera.

But just then Tina nudged him. She saw something moving in the hole.

Sure enough, out came the brown, flat-eared animal. It was smaller than Tina had thought when she saw it in the hole. And behind it came four little animals, bumping and pawing each other, playing together. Their mother turned around and looked at them as if she were counting.

Then she led them down the bank to a rocky little

pool in the stream. They all slipped neatly into the water except one little one who went Splash. Then they paddled around together while the mother swam in a circle around them. "It's a swimming lesson," Tina whispered to Ernest.

Tina forgot her fear. She stared with wonder and delight. She fell in love with those four pretty, playful little ones, and with their mother too who was giving them such a good time in the water. She forgot about her camera. Ernest had to remind her.

The animals were gone from the pool when she got back with the camera. Ernest said they all climbed out on the bank, shook off the water drops, and then the mother led them into the woods. Tina wished she had seen that too.

It was dark by the time Tina and Ernest got home, late for supper. Their father said the animals must have been weasels. Tina's mother looked up WEASEL in the encyclopedia. After studying the pictures they decided that what they had seen were Short-Tailed Canadian Weasels.

Tina's mother read to the others that the weasels eat mice and frogs and are good swimmers. Then she read, "The mother will defend her young with the utmost desperation."

Tina was silent when she heard that, and then sad. "What's the matter, little Peanutina?" asked her father.

Tina sighed and said, "I scared that mother. I have been scaring lots of animal mothers." She pretended to herself that she was a mouse mother or a rabbit mother in her hole, and suddenly a strange creature in goggles looking like a spaceman barged right up to her nest and set off a bright light like a sudden fire. Tina thought how different animals are from peanuts or beads or flour sifters.

The next morning early while Ernest was still sleeping, Tina asked her mother to take her to the park near their house. She wanted to check that the field mouse and her babies were all right.

This time, before she went down the hole she crooned a soothing little song into it so the mouse would know she was a friend:

> Bye baby bunting
> Daddy's gone a-hunting
> To fetch a little rabbit skin
> To wrap his baby bunting in.

"Oh, wow," she thought. "I better not sing that to a rabbit."

The mouse hole was empty. Even the nest was gone, the dried grass scattered.

"Do you think I frightened them so much they ran away from home?" Tina asked her mother.

"Mice grow up very, very fast," said her mother. "I think they grew up and were too big for the nest. I think that's why they're gone."

Tina was glad to hear this, but she was still worried. Now something else was bothering her. The first time she had gone down that mouse hole, it was easy. This time it was hard to wiggle down and hard to get back out too. She felt as if the hole squashed her. But it was the same hole. She wondered what could be the matter with her.

8

Growing

The day after she went down the empty mouse hole Tina had trouble getting her shoes on. Then the seam in her coverall split when she pulled it on. "Why Tina," said her mother. "I do believe you're growing."

Every day from then on Tina seemed to get bigger. She grew too big to get into rabbit holes. And still she kept growing.

Each week she outgrew her clothes. Eggy kept sending bigger ones. Her clothes were getting so big that Eggy needed a sewing machine. After shopping around she chose one with twenty-two attachments. When she wasn't making coveralls for Tina she made clothes for Lucy Dansy and her friends, with buttons and buttonholes, zippers, tucks, ruffles, ruching, appliques, braid, rickrack, smocking, scallops, tassels and many pockets of all sizes.

Eggy was so excited showing off what her machine could do and taking orders that she became proud and happy and gave everybody her business cards.

The picture Tina had taken of the weasel down in the hole was very scary. The weasel's mouth was open wide and there was a look in her eye that seemed to say "I'll chew you to pieces." Tina sent the picture to Slap to give him bad dreams.

All winter, as Tina grew bigger and bigger, she and Ernest went off to the woods on Saturdays. Tina enjoyed seeing her footprints in the snow. She was pleased they were getting larger and larger. She admired the animals' footprints even more than her own. "I make bootprints and so do you," she told Ernest. "But they *really* make footprints."

She learned to tell footprints of rabbits from footprints of weasels. She watched for the little foot tracks of chickadees and the big tracks and flurries in the snow where a hunting owl had swooped down and landed. She took footprint pictures in the sunny snow under the bare tree branches.

The more pictures Tina took, the more she liked taking pictures. And the more she worked the faster she seemed to grow. At home they discussed how fast she was growing and wondered why.

"Maybe it's because of your adventures," said Tina's mother.

"Maybe it's because you work so hard," said Ernest.

"Maybe it's because you wanted to," said her father.

"Maybe it's because it was just time to," said Tina.

They took her to the doctor to ask him why. He tapped Tina's knees with a little hammer. He looked down her throat and in her ears. He told her to read letters on a chart. He took her blood pressure and her temperature. He listened to her heart beating. "You have a fine, healthy little daughter," he said.

"But why is she growing now?" asked Tina's mother.

"Come back a week from today," said the doctor.

When they came back, the doctor sat them in a row in front of his desk and cleared his throat. "The body is very complicated," he said. "It seems she grew because it was time to."

When summer came Lucy Dansy flew up in an airplane for a visit with Tina. She was amazed to see

how big Tina had become. Ernest measured them both in their stocking feet standing back-to-back and announced that Tina was only five inches shorter than Lucy. Then he measured them again with Tina standing on her tiptoes but she still wasn't as tall as Lucy.

"You're big enough," said Lucy. "Big enough is when you can walk with your arms around each other." Every day with their arms around each other Tina and Lucy went to the zoo and made friends with animals and Tina took pictures.

For her birthday Tina got a bigger camera. It came in a brown leather bag with a shoulder strap. Ernest printed on the bag in yellow letters:

E R N E S T I N A

THE ANIMAL PHOTOGRAPHER

"Which are you?" asked Lucy. Are you Ernestina or Peanutina or Tina?"

"They are all the same," said Tina. "They are all me. I am Ernestina The Animal Photographer, but I'm still Peanutina and Tina just the same as always."

At the zoo some of the animals tried to copy Tina and Lucy. Tina got wonderful pictures of a bear cub trying to turn a somersault, a raccoon with its paws over its ears, and a small tan monkey trying its best to turn a cartwheel. She got pictures of animals doing things she couldn't even try to do herself: a seal coming up with a fish in its mouth after a long underwater swim and a flying squirrel gliding down from a high tree branch in the twilight.

One day at breakfast Ernest read out loud a story in the newspaper about the Sasquatch. The paper said that two hikers in the mountains of British Columbia claimed they saw a Sasquatch at the top of a thick pine forest. They said it was gray and looked like a giant furry person. The minute they saw it, it ran back into the woods.

The newspaper reporter had also talked to an expert who said that every few years people thought they saw a Sasquatch or the footprints of a Sasquatch. "But they imagine it," he had told the reporter. "The Sasquatch is not real. It is only a made-up creature in old stories."

All that day at the zoo while she was photographing giraffes and yaks and giggling with Lucy, Tina was also thinking about the Sasquatch. While they were eating supper that night Tina said, "Some day I want to go and photograph the Sasquatch."

"But the Sasquatch is imaginary," said Tina's father.

"How do you know?" asked Tina. "Remember the man at the Bureau of Missing Persons? He said I was imaginary."

Everybody was silent, thinking. Then Tina's mother said, "That is true. You are right, Tina. Very well, some day when you are older and even bigger you may go and try to photograph the Sasquatch. But be very careful."

"Be very brave," said Tina's father.

"Be very lucky," said Ernest.

"Carry peanuts," said Lucy.

Right this minute, while you are reading this, Tina is in the mountains of British Columbia, walking along the top edges of pine forests and watching to catch a glimpse of the Sasquatch.

Her plan is to throw it some peanuts, very gently. While the Sasquatch is picking up the peanuts she will take its picture and run.

It is a daring journey, high above the tops of waterfalls, among black rocks and snowfields. But if the Sasquatch is there Tina will surely bring its picture back home with her.